SPIRIT OF HOPE

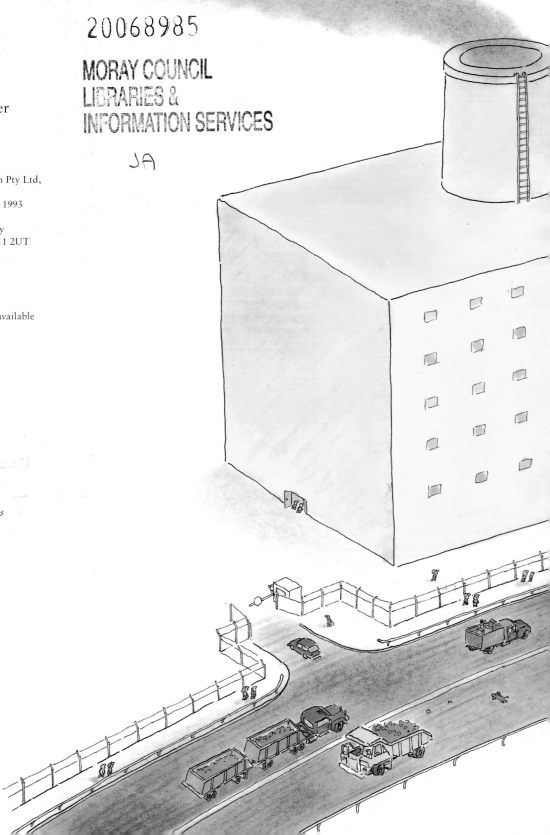

To my mother and father

First Published 1993 by Thomas C. Lothian Pty Ltd,
Melbourne, Australia
Copyright © Blackbird Design Pty Ltd 1993

This edition first published 2000 by
Happy Cat Books, Bradfield, Essex CO11 2UT

Copyright © Bob Graham 2000

A CIP catalogue record for this book is available
from the British Library

ISBN 1 899248 58 7

Printed in Hong Kong

Also by Bob Graham
Greetings from Sandy Beach
Zoltan the Magnificent

*For David Allsop, my thoughts
and my thanks*

SPIRIT OF HOPE

BOB GRAHAM

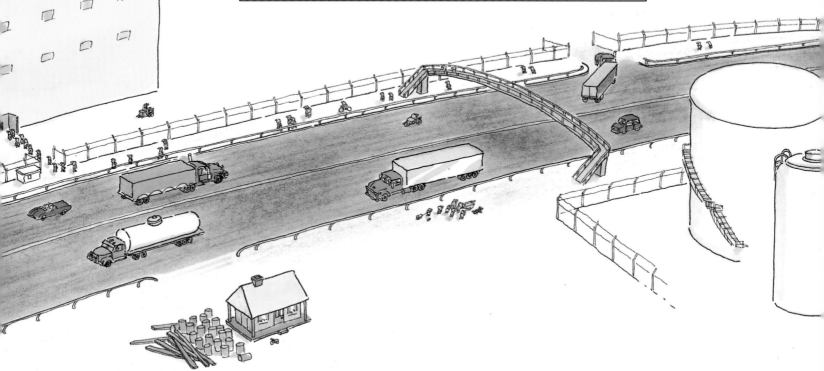

Happy Cat Books

Six days a week the Fairweathers crossed the bridge.
They waved to the passing trucks and the drivers waved back.
Everyone knew the Fairweathers,
and the Fairweathers knew everyone.

Six days a week the Fairweathers said goodbye
to Dad at the factory gate, his lunch
tucked under his arm in a brown paper bag.

Six nights a week Dad returned from work.
The welcome he received was second to none.
Each night he made the journey to the bathroom
on his hands and knees.

Lilly sat up front, then Cecily and Micky, Duggy and Sammy, Jock the dog, Bumper and Thumper, and Trevor the tortoise.

And last of all there was Mary, the youngest Fairweather.

Dad washed off the oil from the factory.
He scrubbed his nails, ten little black crescent moons
in a sea of foam. And he sang, 'The Owl and the
Pussycat went to sea in a beautiful pea green boat . . .'

Then Mum sang, 'Little Mary Fairweather dancing in the snow. Wiggle-wiggle-wiggle. Go, go, go.'

And Dad did his bird calls. 'Hopeless,' yelled Micky. 'Let's be a Ship at Sea,' they called.

A chair was put on the kitchen table. 'Who's the Captain tonight?' called Lilly. 'Sammy can be Captain,' Mum replied.' 'Say it, Dad, *say it!*' they yelled.

'Full steam ahead,' said Dad.
'Let's imagine our house is a ship at sea, chugging along
in the darkness. Listen to the engines.
Pom-da-pom-da-pom.'
Sammy sat up in the chair with the Captain's hat on,
and steered the house to Faraway and Exotic places.

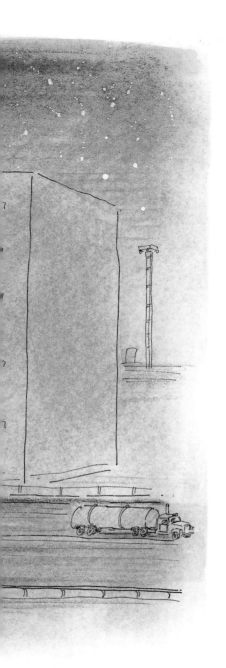

Then Lilly and Cecily, Micky and Duggy,
Sammy and Mary would climb
into bed and go to sleep,
with the sound of the big trucks
rolling by in the night.

The seventh day was picnic day on the docks, with plum jam sandwiches, ginger beer and fruit cake. They heard the cries of the gulls and the slap of water on the hulls of the ships.

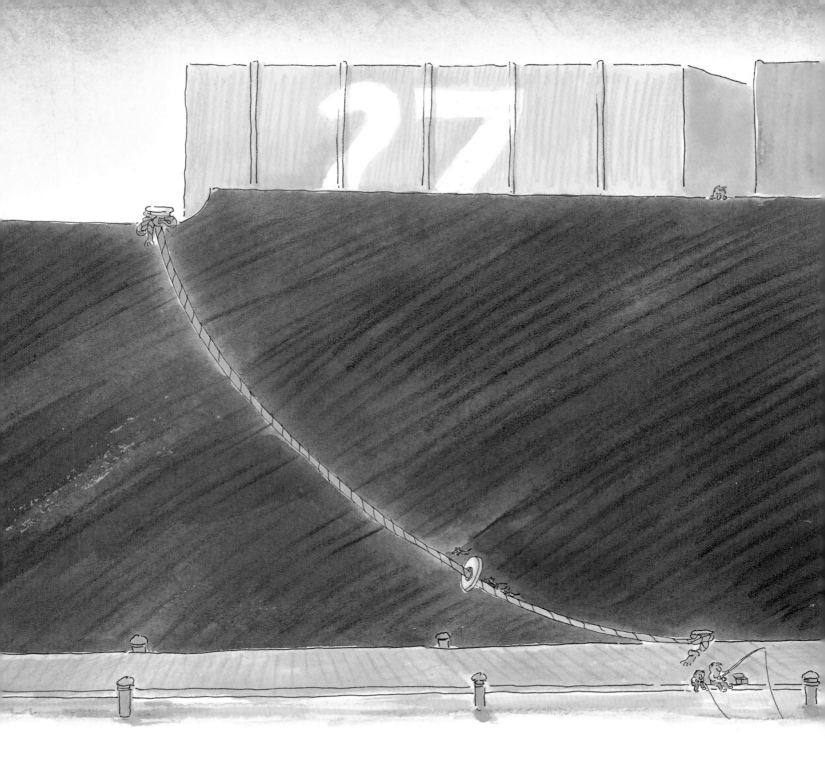

One day they saw sailors from a faraway port.
'Join us for our picnic,' called Dad. 'What is the
name of your ship?'
'*Spirit of Hope,*' the sailors shouted.

As the Fairweathers returned home from their picnic, it seemed that their house was an island where the sun always shone.

But that evening everything changed. There was a knock at the door.

'Are you the Fairweathers?' asked one of the men.
'Yes,' replied Dad. 'Come in.'
'No, thank you,' said the man. 'We have come to inform you that you must move.'
Twelve faces stared at him.
'*And soon,*' he added.

'Why must we move?' Lilly asked.
'To make way for a factory,' Dad replied.
'A factory? Where?' said Cecily.
'Here,' said Mum pointing to the floor.
'What for?' asked Micky.
'For matchsticks,' replied Dad.
'A factory to make matchsticks,' Mum repeated.
'And what will happen to our dear little house?'
There was silence.
'Matchsticks,' Dad replied, and put
his head in his hands.

That night there were no Captains steering the ship
from the kitchen table.
A gloomy silence hung over the Fairweather house.

'We must not despair,' said Mum.
'We must keep up a Spirit of Hope.'

'No matter what happens, at least we are together.
Tomorrow we shall look for a new house.'

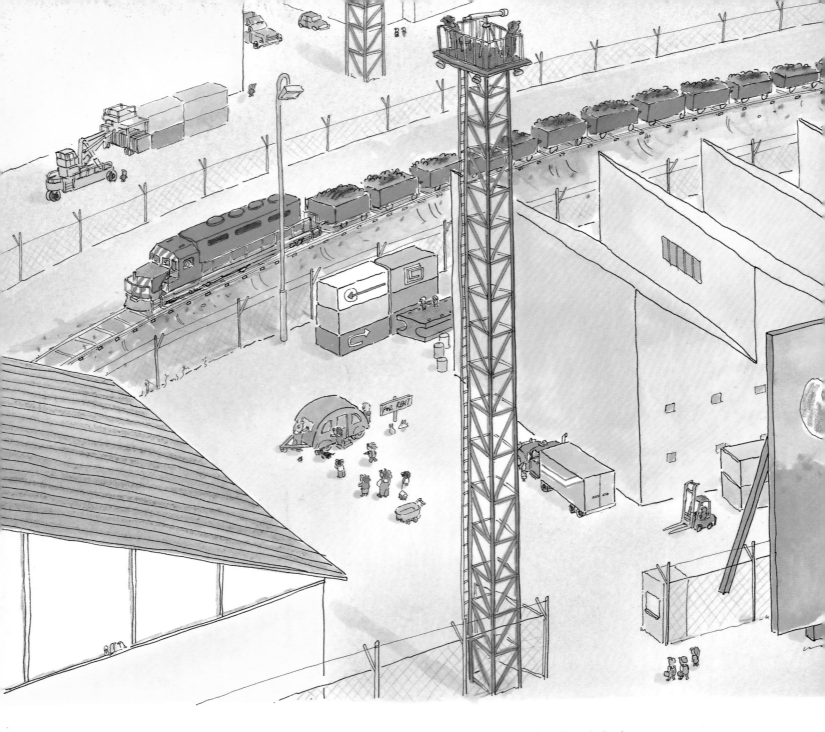

All the next week the Fairweathers searched with hope. Their friends all searched too. All they found were warehouses, factories, goods yards and one small caravan out near the railway.

'Too small,' said Dad. 'No grass for the rabbits,' said Cecily.

'We'll try again next week,' said Mum.
Mary said nothing.

The following week the Fairweathers searched in despair,
until they could search no more.
'I feel,' said Dad, 'that we are adrift on a sea of trouble.'

'Well *I* feel,' said Mum, looking at Mary,
'that the answer to our troubles is closer than we thought.
Quick, Mary, we have no time to lose.'

'What are we going to do?' asked the children.
'No time to explain,' replied Mum.
Mary's house bumped along all the way home.

'It must be something to do with Mary,' said Lilly.
'No, it's *nothing* to do with Mary,' said Cecily.
'Hurry!' called Mum. 'Bring those planks over here.'

'Yes, it is Mary,' said Micky.
'And her toy house,' added Duggy.

'Roll those drums over here—
Hurry,' cried Mum.

The excavator clawed its way to the corner of their house.
'We're too late,' shouted Dad. 'All is lost.'
'We need our friends,' yelled Mum.
'Help!' cried the Fairweathers.

And the Fairweathers' friends came from everywhere.

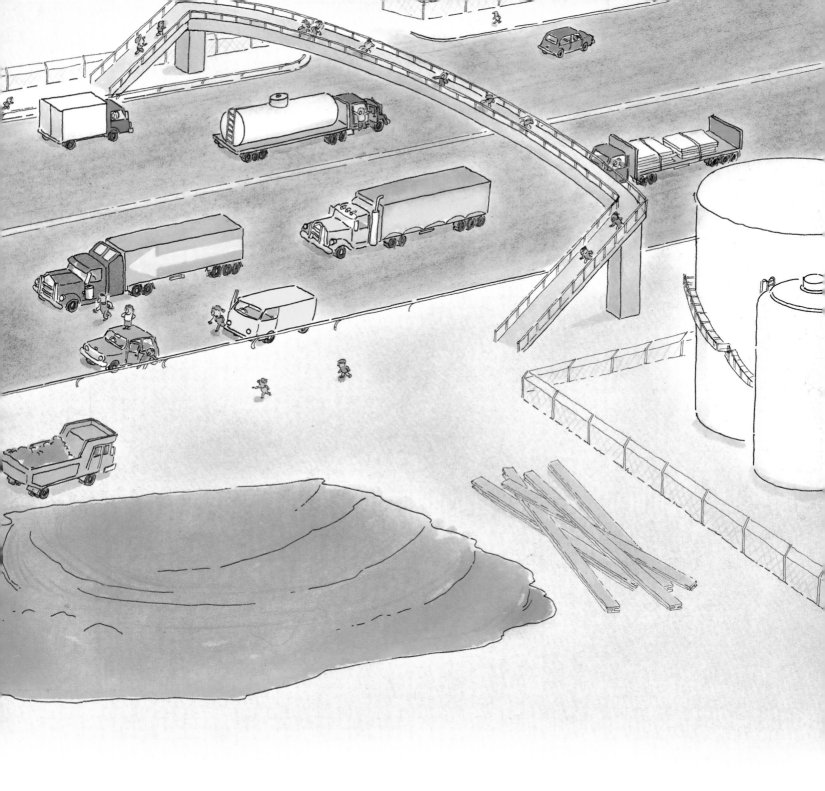

Mary Fairweather watched everything, her toy house
dangling from its string.

With a mighty wrench, the house
left the ground and swung
high in the air.

It turned three times on its
cable, then became a house
on wheels.

'I shall call our house "Spirit of Hope",' shouted Dad,
and dipped his brush into a tin of black paint.

The Fairweathers' house bumped along the road
all the way to the docks.

Now, even on the darkest night, there is a light glowing at the end of the pier. The house seems to be pulling gently at its moorings, wanting to slip away with the tide.

'Who will be Captain tonight?' ask Cecily, Lilly,
Micky, Duggy and Sammy.

'Mary,' says Dad.